Lisa Stevenson

Knickerless Nicola

Knickerless Nicola

Kara May
Illustrated by Doffy Weir

MACMILLAN CHILDREN'S BOOKS

For Helen and Anna

First published 1989 by
MACMILLAN CHILDREN'S BOOKS
A division of Macmillan Publishers Limited
London and Basingstoke
Associated companies throughout the world

Picturemac edition published 1991

ISBN 0-333-55132-X

A CIP catalogue record for this book is available from
the British Library

Printed in Hong Kong

Nicola was having breakfast.
Suddenly, she did something she had
never done before.

She climbed down from her chair . . .

... and took off her knickers!
She waved them up and down.
"Look, Mum!" she said. "I've got a flag!"

"Don't be silly, Nicola. Your knickers aren't a flag.
Put them on and keep them on!" said Mum.

But Nicola took no notice.
She kept on taking off her knickers.
She took them off at the oddest times,
in the oddest places!

When they went to Gran's for tea, she whirled them
round and round.
"Look at my windmill, Mum!"
she said.

When they went to visit next door's baby, she took off her knickers and threw them in the air.

"Look, Mum!" she giggled. "Look what's sitting on the lampshade!"

When they went to the park,
she put them on her head.
"Hey, Mum, do you like my hat?"
she cried.

"Why won't you keep your knickers on?" asked Mum.
"'Cos I don't want to!" grinned Nicola.
"Well," said Mum, "they're almost worn out.
If you *really* don't want to wear them,
we may as well throw them away.
Shall we do that?"

"Yes, let's," said Nicola.

"I'll keep this pair," said Mum.
"I'll use them for a duster."

Nicola couldn't stop laughing.
Upstairs and down she ran, chanting:
"Nicola's got no knickers on,
Nicola's got no knickers on!
Ha! Ha! Ha!"

Knickerless Nicola was very pleased
with herself. But not for long!
When she went outside, into next door's garden . . .

the wind felt very cold.

"Brrrr!" she shivered.
"I'm freeeeezing!"

Then, at Gran's –
"Ouch!" she squawked. "This sofa's prickly!"

She didn't cheer up
when they went to the park.
"I don't like that swing!
It's hard and splintery!"

"I want to go home!"
grumbled Nicola.

The next day, they went on a bus.
Nicola stomped off.
"That seat was hot and sticky! Yuk!"
she said.

"Hurry up," said Mum,
"I want to do the shopping."

"Ouch! Ouwwww! Mum!" cried Nicola.
"Now what?" said Mum.
"I slipped! It hurts!"
Mum helped her up. "I need a cup
of tea!" she sighed.

"Can I have an ice-cream?"
asked Nicola.

They went and found a café.

"Don't you want to sit down?" asked Mum.
But Nicola didn't want to sit down.
Her bottom was much too sore.
"I'm fed up!" she said.
"I'm fed up with the wind blowing up my legs.
I'm fed up with sitting on prickly sofas.
I'm fed up with splintery swings and sticky
bus seats.
I'm fed up with standing up 'cos I can't sit down!
What I need is some *knickers*.
Shall we go and buy some?"
"Yes, let's," said Mum.

"I like these, Mum.
They're just right!"
said Nicola.
Mum bought her three more
pairs, all with butterflies on.

Nicola carried
the bag herself.
"I think I'll sing a knicker song,"
she said.
"Well, sing it very softly,"
said Mum.
Very softly, Nicola began
to sing:
"I've got my knickers on,
I've got my knickers on,
. . . And I'm going to keep them on."

And she did.

Other Picturemacs you will enjoy

Henry and the Frights Terence Blacker
Jack and Nancy Quentin Blake
A Rose for Pinkerton Steven Kellogg
Pookins Gets her Way Helen Lester/Lynn Munsinger
There's Something Spooky in My Attic Mercer Mayer
Henrietta Goose Abigail Pizer
Alistair Underwater Marilyn Sadler and Roger Bollen

For a complete list of Picturemac titles write to:

Macmillan Children's Books,
18–21 Cavaye Place, London SW10 9PG